CENW

We hope you enjoy this book.
Please return or renew it by the due date.
You can renew it at **www.norfolk.gov.uk/libraries**
or by using our free library app. Otherwise you can
phone **0344 800 8020** - please have your library
card and pin ready.
You can sign up for email reminders too.

PEACE MAKER

Malorie BLACKMAN

With illustrations by Matthew Griffin

Barrington Stoke

www.malorieblackman.co.uk

For Neil and Lizzy
With love, as always

First published in 2016 in Great Britain by
Barrington Stoke Ltd
18 Walker Street, Edinburgh, EH3 7LP

www.barringtonstoke.co.uk

This story was first published in a different form in
Fantastic Space Stories (Transworld, 1994)

Text © 1994 Oneta Malorie Blackman
Illustrations © 2016 Matthew Griffin

The moral right of Oneta Malorie Blackman and Matthew Griffin to be
identified as the author and illustrator of this work has been asserted in
accordance with the Copyright, Designs and Patents Act, 1988

A CIP catalogue record for this book is available
from the British Library upon request

ISBN: 978-1-78112-561-8

Printed in China by Leo

CONTENTS

CHAPTER 1
STORY

"Michela Corbin, what did I just say?"

The class began to snigger. I looked up in dismay. There, right in front of my desk, was Teacher Faber. I stared up at her and blinked with confusion. I hadn't even seen her coming! I tried to cover my screen with my hand, but the teacher was too fast for me. She snatched up my screen and started to read the story I'd been writing. I groaned. I was in deep, *deep* trouble. Again!

"Michela Corbin, you are supposed to be writing an essay on section 4.15 of the Peace

Treaty between the Alliance and the Others. Not this ... this ... *this!*" Teacher Faber waved my screen under my nose.

"I'm sorry. I'll delete it." I grabbed for my screen. Teacher Faber snatched it back.

"Let us take a look at what has kept you so busy," the teacher said. Her tone was dripping with sarcasm. "Are you ready for this, class?" she asked.

"I spun around, fast as a spitting cobra. Davin lunged at me with her laz-sword. I swung my weapon down to parry her thrust. The sound of laser beam on laser beam was a musical zing. With a roar of fury, Davin whipped her laz-sword up towards my head. I ducked and stepped back. I didn't want to hurt her, but one touch from the laz-sword would be lethal – and I wasn't prepared to die. I ..."

Teacher Faber stopped reading, but not before my face was on fire. Half the class were

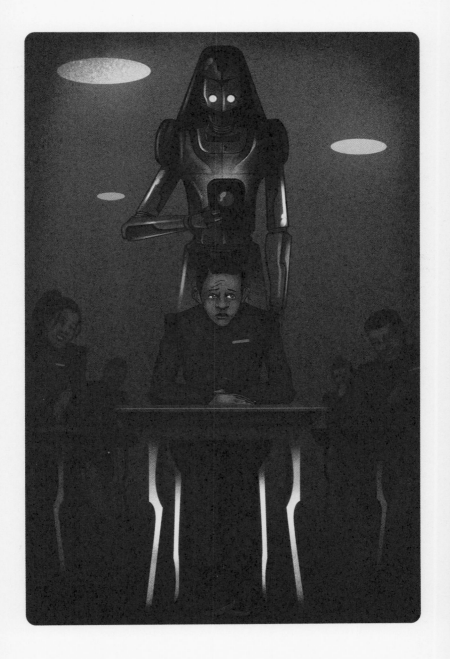

in fits of laughter. The other half were glaring at me.

"This tish-tosh is not just nonsense, it's dangerous nonsense," Teacher Faber said. "I told you the last time that you'd had your final warning. Now you'll go on report. Again."

"Oh please, you can't," I begged. "My mother will go nuts! I'll do the essay. I'll stay behind and work late. I'll ..."

Teacher Faber broke in. "Not another word," she said. "You're on report and that's final. And I shall make sure that your mother sees this ... this story of yours."

My blood ran icy cold. "You can't do that ..." I whispered.

"Watch me," Teacher Faber said. "I don't know what's wrong with you, Michela. You persist with writing these absurd stories ..."

"They're adventures," I protested. "They're just made up ..."

"You humans are supposed to abhor violence of any kind – even in stories," Teacher Faber said. "And yet, Michela, you insist on reading forbidden books like *Treasure Island* and *The Hunger Games*. And then you write this kind of fantastical, dangerous foolishness."

It wasn't my fault I read forbidden books. If they weren't forbidden in the first place, then I wouldn't get into trouble for reading them! My mother owned an impressive collection of books from the past 200 years. Most of them were fiction and most of them were now forbidden.

My mother kept the books locked up in glass cases in a room she called the Library, and it had taken me ages to get at them without her knowing. She called them "a good investment" – whatever that meant. I called them a good read. I didn't see the point in owning books if you didn't read them. The trouble was, Mother didn't see it like that. She'd caught me with my nose in one of her books more than once. The last time, Mother threatened to burn them all if she caught me with just one of them again. So instead of reading, I'd taken to writing my own stories – but that seemed to get me into even worse trouble.

"I won't read or write stories any more," I pleaded. "Please don't report me."

Teacher Faber keyed in some commands on the console. Her fingers moved so fast that they were a blur.

"It is done," Teacher Faber said as she moved away. "I have sent a full report to Commander Newton and to your mother."

I scowled at her. Rotten, snake-brained weasel robot! Then I groaned. What was my mother going to say?

CHAPTER 2
PEACE MAKER

"Teacher Faber sent me yet another demerit report on you today," Mother said.

"Mother, I can explain ..."

Mother flopped down into her favourite chair and kicked off her shoes. "Michela, I don't want to hear it." She sighed. "I've reasoned with you, pleaded with you, argued with you until I'm blue in the face."

"It was only a story, Mother," I mumbled.

"A story!" she said. "Why can't you write stories about proper subjects? What's wrong with peace and diplomacy and friendship? Why must you revel in swords and lasers and violence?"

"I don't," I said, and my blood started to boil. "They're only stories, Mother ..."

"They're a way of thinking. They're a way of *being*," my mother replied. "You persist in embarrassing me in front of my co-workers. What would your father say if he was still alive?"

And with that one single argument, Mother squashed any protest I was about to make.

An uncomfortable silence filled the room.

At last, Mother chose to break it. "Michela, have you been re-coding your Peace Maker?" she asked.

"Of course not!" I blustered.

After the *Treasure Island* thing happened, Mother sent for Doctor Bevan to have my Peace Maker checked out. Everyone had a Peace Maker attached to the inside of their left arm on their 11th birthday. Everyone had one, and we had them for life. The Peace Maker was a small, grey disc which looked a bit like one of those old-fashioned buttons people used to use to fasten their clothes.

Doctor Bevan explained that the Peace Maker would inhibit my behaviour – it would make sure that the non-aggression we'd all been taught for the past 100 years was more than just a lesson. The Peace Maker was supposed to make sure that it was physically impossible for us humans to be aggressive. No more wars, no more fights. We couldn't hurt each other any more.

Only it didn't stop there. Books and films that used to be classics had now been banned. And the list of things seen as signs of aggression grew longer and longer every day. Things like talking, laughing and singing too loudly – and as I do all three, I'm always on report! Take last East Day, for example. We had Hal-C-Yon flowers from Rig-4 for pudding. Hal-C-Yon flowers are most people's favourite food, a treat we only have one day a year because they're so difficult to grow and expensive to buy. Jen Peters tried to pinch mine and because I protested I was put on report and hauled up in front of Mother. Again.

"How come it's all right for Jen to steal my food but it's not all right for me to stop her?" I demanded.

"Jen was wrong too," Mother said. "But you were more wrong! Your reaction could have led to violence. And as my daughter, Michela, you should know better."

And that was the problem. I was always letting Mother down.

Mother shook her head sadly. "Why do you do it? I read your story, Michela. Is that really what's in your head – in spite of everything I've tried to teach you?"

"It was just a story, Mother," I whispered unhappily.

"And the part where you were fighting with the laz-sword?" Mother asked.

"I put that in because it's the only weapon I've seen pictures of," I said.

"You told me that you wanted to train in Kendo to teach you balance and grace," Mother said. "But it's clear that all you want to do is pretend that you're fighting with a real weapon. I forbid you to practise that so-called sport from now on."

"But it's the only thing I'm any good at," I protested. "Don't take that away from me."

Mother sighed and folded her arms.

'Please ... Not that as well,' I thought desperately.

"That's enough," Mother said. "You're not to practise Kendo any more and that's final."

From the harsh, closed look on her face, I knew she meant it.

"And you can go to Doctor Bevan right this minute and get your Peace Maker checked out," Mother said. "If I find out that you *have* been tampering with it ..."

CHAPTER 3
CAPTAIN

"CON ONE! CON ONE! Captain Corbin to the bridge immediately. Captain Corbin to the bridge."

The alert stopped Mother in the middle of her sentence. She slipped her shoes back on and within seconds she was out the door. I stared after her. What was going on? What had happened to take us from Con Four – our usual state – to Con One? Con One was only used for extreme danger. Usually the Cons moved up one by one – not in one big jump from Four to One.

Mother was the captain of our ship and so I was used to her being called away at a moment's notice. At first it was exciting to have such an important mother – captain of the *Kitabu*, one of the most important ships in the Alliance fleet. But in the last few weeks the excitement had ebbed away to leave something else in its place – something less noble. I hardly ever saw her. And it seemed to me that Mother was always Captain Corbin first. Being my mum came a long way down the list of her priorities. I didn't want to feel the way I did, but I couldn't help it.

"Come on, Michela," I muttered, pulling myself together. "What am I going to do now?" I glanced down at my Peace Maker. Whatever the emergency was, it had saved me from a trip to Doctor Bevan and some *real* trouble.

"What's going on?" I asked out loud.

There was only one way to find out. I left the room and headed up to the ship's bridge. Maybe I could sneak in without Mother seeing me.

CHAPTER 4
ALIEN

The moment I stepped onto the bridge, I gasped, then froze. There, right in front of the *Kitabu*, was the biggest ship I'd ever seen. It must have had some kind of sensor-jamming device to appear before us like this without any warning.

There was no way anyone was going to throw me off the bridge. All eyes were on the colossal ship before us.

"Officer Cash, activate the universal decoder. Open a channel," Mother said. She was standing before the viewer on the bridge, and her expression was solemn. "This is

Captain Corbin of the Alliance ship, *Kitabu*. We come in peace. Our mission is to open trade routes across this sector. Do you understand?"

Each time we had an encounter with a new ship, Mother – or Commander Newton, her second-in-command – had to say the same words. The idea was that the new ship would analyse the words, so that any further communication between us and them could be translated. That's the way our universal decoder worked.

Everyone on the bridge looked tense. This was always the worst moment of dealing with a new ship and a new civilisation. We never knew quite how they would react.

After a few moments, the ship disappeared off the screen and was replaced by the face and upper body of one of the new ship's crew. And such a face, I'd never seen before. My breath caught in my throat and refused to budge. The alien's face had only one eye in the middle of its forehead like a cyclops. Its nose was a series of huge ridges across its face and its lips were similar enough to human lips to be recognisable. But the thing that made me stare without blinking was the alien's skin. It was transparent. I could see grey blood running along tiny canals in its body. I could see the tops of two organs, one on either side of its upper body, contracting and expanding. These two organs had to be the alien's hearts. The whole thing looked strange – and totally weird!

"This is Captain Corbin of the Alliance ship, *Kitabu*. We come in peace. Do you understand?" Mother repeated. She didn't bat an eyelid at the look of the thing before her.

"I am Flack-Tor, a Chamra knight. And yes, I understand," the alien replied. "You have entered our sector without permission and you must pay the price."

"The price?" Mother asked. Her voice was sharp.

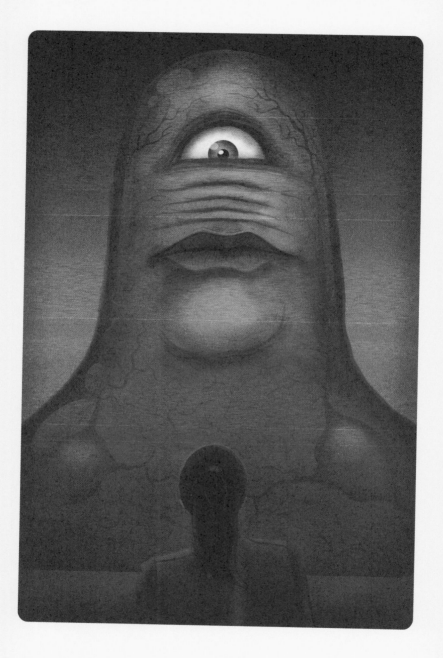

"The price," Flack-Tor said. "Our ships are now at war."

"We were not aware that we required permission," Mother said. "My ship is the first Alliance ship to enter this sector. We in the Alliance are peaceful. We meant no harm."

"Harm or not, it is Chamra law," Flack-Tor said. "We are now at war."

"We will not fight you," said Mother.

"You have no choice," said Flack-Tor.

"We will leave this sector and never return," Mother said.

"You cannot retreat," Flack-Tor told her. "Your path lies ahead."

Silence.

"Comms down," Mother said. That way she could hear what Flack-Tor had to say but he couldn't hear her. "Officer Dopp, what's the maximum speed of this unknown ship?" she asked.

"Velocity 5, our sensors say," the officer replied.

"Comms up," Mother said, and two-way communications resumed. "Flack-Tor, I must repeat, we in the Alliance are peace-loving," Mother said. "We are peace-makers, not war-makers. We will not fight with you. Our ship can travel more than twice as fast as your craft. I will use that speed to retreat so that our meeting does not end in violence."

"Run if you must," Flack-Tor said. "But I will spend the rest of my days searching the galaxy for you. I will hunt you down. I have issued the challenge. It is not yours to reject."

"But this makes no sense. Why won't you let us leave? Why must we fight?" Mother asked. An edge crept into her voice.

"It is our way," said Flack-Tor. "And if you leave, it is not only our two ships that will be at war. My people on Chamra will be at war with your Alliance." There was a pause before he added, "As you did not know you had broken our laws, I am also bound to inform you of another option."

"I'm listening," Mother said. Her voice was eager now.

"You may send your champion to fight the best knight on my ship," Flack-Tor said.

Mother's shoulders slumped. "We have many champions," she said, "but not that kind. We are not fighters – none of us."

"Then how do you propose we go on with our combat?" Flack-Tor asked.

"I propose we don't go on at all," Mother said. "No one on this ship will fight you. It's against everything we believe in." Her fingers touched the necklace that Father had given her years before. It was her only sign of nerves. I could almost hear her thinking, her face was so intent. "I have another option of my own to suggest."

"Then suggest it," the alien barked.

"We surrender," Mother said.

CHAPTER 5
SURRENDER

Commander Newton sat up straight in his chair. Officer Cash took a deep breath. No one else on the bridge moved.

Flack-Tor's face was as still and as impossible to read as a stone. He beckoned to one of his own crew, and they whispered together for a few moments.

Flack-Tor turned back to the screen. "We do not know the word 'surrender'. Explain."

"It means we admit defeat. We submit. We yield. We will stop resisting and give ourselves over to you," Mother said. "We will not fight."

Flack-Tor smiled. "Your Alliance is worthless. A Chamra baby has more courage than your ship's entire crew. You will not surrender. You will stand and fight. Or you will stand and die. The choice is yours. You have 50 seconds to prepare."

Flack-Tor's face disappeared from the screen and was replaced by his ship.

CHAPTER 6
HUG

"Officer Cash, open another channel," Mother said after a pause. "I've got to try and reason with them."

"They're not responding, Captain," Officer Cash said.

"Keep trying."

"What do we do, Captain?" Commander Newton asked.

"If they don't answer ... we prepare to die," Mother said. She was still staring at the screen. "We will not put the Alliance in danger. *We will not fight*."

"We could leave this sector," Commander Newton suggested.

"No. We're not going to run," said Mother. "We cannot let this become a full-blown war between the Alliance and the Chamra nation. We must try to appeal to them, but if not ..." Mother didn't say any more. She didn't have to.

I stared at her. Would she really let us all die, without a fight? I looked around the bridge and saw that everyone had the same steely look as Mother on their faces. I had my answer.

I looked down at my Peace Maker. How I wished I hadn't tampered with it. The others on the bridge were prepared to do as their captain said and die rather than go against their beliefs. Me? I wanted to fight. And the feeling was so strong that it scared me. What could I do? I was only 13.

"Mother, can I ...?" I began.

Mother's head whipped around. "Michela, get off the bridge. You're not supposed to be up here." She didn't even let me finish.

I looked at her. And she looked back at me, with worry and sadness on her face. At that moment, I knew there was no hope. We were going to die. I turned away. Mother called me back and hugged me. I clung to her, surprised by the warmth of her hug, but all too soon it ended.

"Go to our room," Mother said kindly. "I'll join you later."

After a pause, I left the bridge without another word – but I didn't go back to our room. It was too late to wonder what I would've done and how I would've felt if I hadn't tampered with my Peace Maker. The point was, I had. And if Flack-Tor of the Chamra wanted a fighter, then he would get one.

CHAPTER 7
CHALLENGE

"Shuttle pod 3, identify yourself. That is an order." Commander Newton's voice boomed around the shuttle pod.

I didn't answer. I couldn't answer – not yet. Not until I had finished re-jigging the codes and the force field cycle. Once that was done, I opened a channel to the alien ship.

"This is shuttle pod 3. I wish to speak to Flack-Tor," I said over and over again, in the hope that someone would answer me.

"Michela? What do you think you're doing?" Mother's face appeared on the screen to my left. Her expression was shocked and her voice burned with fury. "Michela, bring shuttle pod 3 back to this ship at once."

"I can't, Mother," I said. "Please don't try to stop me."

"Officer Cash, lock onto that shuttle pod and bring it back," Mother commanded.

"I can't, Captain," the officer replied. "The codes have been changed. We no longer have any control over that pod."

"Then use the tracking beam to bring her back," Mother snapped.

"Sorry, Captain," Officer Cash replied after a few moments. "The pod's force field has been re-programmed to cycle at random every few seconds. I can't get a lock."

Mother turned her focus back to me. "Michela, bring that pod back now and I promise we'll say no more about it," she said. "Running away from this ship isn't the answer. Your pod can't outrun the Chamra. Your place is on this ship – no matter what happens."

I stared at her. I couldn't believe it. Did she really think I was trying to run away, to escape the *Kitabu*'s fate? Is that what she thought of me?

"Bye, Mother," I said. I switched off the screen and carried on transmitting my message to Flack-Tor.

Then, without warning, his image appeared on my screen. I swallowed hard.

"Flack-Tor." I coughed to clear my throat. "Flack-Tor, I am Michela Corbin of the Alliance ship, *Kitabu*. I am here to accept your challenge."

Flack-Tor's eye narrowed. "You are a human?"

"Yes."

"You are a knight?"

"Not exactly."

"You are a warrior."

"Not quite," I said. "But it doesn't matter what I am. I accept your challenge."

There was a hush like death. Then every part of me, every drop of blood in my body, froze. The next thing I knew I was standing right in front of Flack-Tor.

"W-what happened?" I whispered

Flack-Tor spoke to me, but I didn't understand. I shook my head. I felt something being injected into my ear. It was uncomfortable for a moment but it didn't hurt.

"Our conveyor beam brought you aboard our ship." Flack-Tor spoke and this time I could understand every word. "I wanted to see you for myself."

"Well, here I am. What happens now?" I asked.

For the first time, the enormity of what I was doing struck me. This was for real. And, unlike in one of my stories, I wouldn't be coming back. I'd never see my mother or the *Kitabu* crew again, but I would make sure they were safe and free. And, because of that, I felt so strange, so *calm*, so clear.

I was in the middle of an *adventure*. This was happening. It wasn't a fantasy I'd written out on my screen. It wasn't a dream in my head. It was real.

"You will fight my ship's champion knight," Flack-Tor told me.

"Are you the captain of this ship?" I asked.

"I am."

"Then I will fight no one but you," I said. My voice was steady and quiet.

Flack-Tor stared at me. Then he started to smile. I wondered if the look on his face meant he was impressed. Perhaps it was just his dinner repeating on him.

"Your challenge is accepted," Flack-Tor said. "Let us go to the arena."

I swallowed hard. I was pushing my luck, but there was one more thing. "I'd like our fight broadcast to the *Kitabu*. I want my ... Captain Corbin and all the *Kitabu* crew to see our contest."

"Agreed," Flack-Tor said. "You will now come with me. We will dress you as a Chamra knight and you must select your weapon."

CHAPTER 8
ARMOUR

The arena was a small circular pit about five metres across and filled with something that felt like Earth sand, only it was dark green in colour. Other aliens like Flack-Tor sat around the arena. Funny, but they didn't look so weird any more. In fact, they looked noble. I supposed that, if you had enough time – and the right frame of mind – you could get used to anything.

Shouts and cheers filled the air and in walked Flack-Tor. He was dressed as I was, in an outfit that covered him from neck-to-toe.

It was like an Earth suit of armour, but the Chamra kind was really flexible. It was very light and comfortable.

In his hand Flack-Tor held a ball that hung from a chain on a stick. For my weapon, I'd chosen the closest thing to a laz-sword I could find. This one was solid metal but with a laser-sharp edge. It wouldn't have made much difference what I'd chosen. I had never faced a real opponent in my life. An instructor robot had been my Kendo teacher. But a robot would be no match for a skilled knight with Chamra weapons.

Flack-Tor stepped into the arena. The crowd fell silent. I looked around. Was Mother watching me now? I hoped she was. If she was, what was she thinking? I would have given anything to know. Here I stood, in front of Flack-Tor – but it still felt as if I was failing my mother. If only I'd left my Peace Maker alone – how much easier life would've been.

Flack-Tor raised his weapon and moved towards me. I let instinct take over and I backed away and raised my sword between us. Flack-Tor and I stepped in a circle around each other. My heart was about to explode from my chest. I could hear the blood roaring and rushing in my ears like a stormy sea.

Flack-Tor lunged at me. I was too terrified to even cry out, and I leaped back. I stared at him, took a deep breath, then another. Then I relaxed my grip on the sword. I'd been holding it so tight that my fingers were turning numb. I stood up straight. I'd made up my mind. I might lose, but Flack-Tor would know he'd been in a fight!

The battle between us lasted longer than I thought it would – a good 45 seconds. And that wasn't the only surprise.

I won.

My heart was pounding, my head was throbbing, and my palms were sweating. But I won.

My first two moves blocked Flack-Tor's attempts to lunge at me. With my third sword stroke, I knocked his weapon out of his hand. It sailed up into the air away from us. I thrust forward until the point of my sword touched Flack-Tor's body. He didn't say a word. No one around us moved. The silence roared in my ears. I watched him, he watched me. Then I threw my sword down on the ground.

I waited, unsure what to do next.

CHAPTER 9
FRIENDS

There was a long pause. No one moved.

Then, without warning, Flack-Tor tilted back his head and laughed. The others around the arena joined in, until the air was filled with the sound of their laughter.

"Is that it?" I asked, confused. "What happens now?"

"Well done, little one. You have passed our test."

"Test?"

"You accepted my challenge. You fought, but you did not kill," Flack-Tor said.

"Test?" Then I realised. "You let me win! But ... but I could have killed you." I stared at him.

Flack-Tor beckoned to one of his crew. The crew member left his seat and came into the arena. He picked up the weapon I had just thrown on the ground. Before I could stop him, before I could even cry out, he lunged at Flack-Tor. I watched, wide-eyed with horror as the sword blade passed right through Flack-Tor's flesh. The captain didn't even flinch. In fact, he laughed again at the look on my face.

Then I saw what had happened. All the canals filled with grey liquid and one of Flack-Tor's hearts had moved out of the way of the sword. They had all shifted above or below the blade.

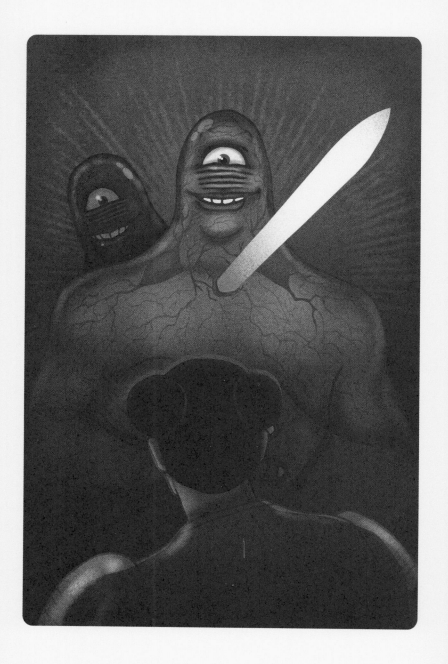

"Every part of me has a life of its own," Flack-Tor explained. "And they could sense the sword coming."

"But I don't understand," I said. "Why this test?"

"We Chamra have to choose our friends with care," Flack-Tor said. "We are a peaceful race. We do not want aggressors as friends. We do not want aggressors using our trade routes. But we do not want cowards as our friends either. You showed that you were prepared to fight for what you believed in, no matter what might happen to you – but you didn't kill me. You could have done but you didn't."

"Because killing is wrong," I said.

"If you believe that, then why did you accept the challenge?" Flack-Tor asked.

"Because … because sometimes … sometimes you have to take a stand, even if you think you're going to lose." I frowned. "And I couldn't let you destroy our ship and kill our crew, not when I thought I could do something about it. How could I sit back and not do anything?"

"You are indeed very brave," Flack-Tor said. "And bravery to us is everything."

'Brave …' I thought. 'Would Mother see it that way?'

But then another, stranger thought came to me. By refusing to kill, but not running away, didn't Mother do just the same thing as I was doing now? Mother was just as brave as Flack-Tor. Only I'd never realised it before.

"Can they still see me on the *Kitabu?*" I asked.

"Yes."

I turned to the viewer. "Mother, I need to see Doctor Bevan," I said. "I *did* recode my Peace Maker, but don't worry. I won't tamper with it any more."

"Peace Maker?" Flack-Tor said.

So I explained.

And after I had explained about the Peace Maker, Flack-Tor was silent for a time.

Then he said, "But you have proven that you do not need to wear such a device. You were prepared to fight and die for your ship and your comrades, but you weren't prepared to kill where there was no need. You showed compassion. That was all we needed to see."

I looked down at my Peace Maker ... and wondered.

"I will escort you to the bridge of my ship," Flack-Tor said. "You will be sent back to your ship from there."

As we walked back, I turned to him. "Flack-Tor, may I keep my weapon and armour?" I asked. "To remember you by?"

Flack-Tor nodded. "Will you be punished when you return to your ship?" he asked.

"I should think so." I sighed. Thoughts of endless essays to write and lectures to listen to filled my head.

"Is there no one on your ship who will be proud of you?" Flack-Tor asked.

"I ... I don't know." I shrugged.

Somehow, somehow I thought that Mother would understand. But even if she didn't, it wouldn't matter.

"I'm proud of myself," I said at last. "And that's enough."

MALORIE BLACKMAN has written lots of fantastic "techno-thriller" novels, including ...

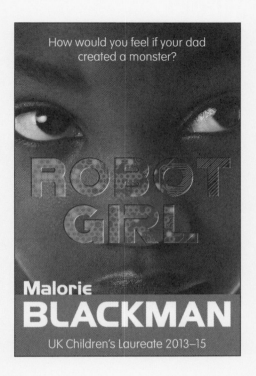

How would you feel if your dad created a monster?

ROBOT GIRL

Malorie
BLACKMAN

UK Children's Laureate 2013–15

Claire's dad is a top inventor. But he keeps his work secret from his family. When at last he reveals his latest project, Claire's life begins to fall apart.

How would you feel if your dad created a monster?

www.barringtonstoke.co.uk